Bugging Miss Bannigan

Franzeska G. Ewart

illustrated by Georgie Birkett

■ SCHOLASTIC

To Tayyibah and Ayesha, with thanks

Scholastic Children's Books,
Commonwealth House, 1-19 New Oxford Street,
London, WC1A 1NU, UK
a division of Scholastic Ltd
London ~ New York ~ Toronto ~ Sydney ~ Auckland
Mexico City ~ New Delhi ~ Hong Kong

First published by Scholastic Ltd, 2003

Text copyright © Franzeska G. Ewart, 2003
Illustrations copyright © Georgie Birkett, 2003

ISBN 0 439 97848 3

Printed and bound by Cox and Wyman Ltd, Reading, Berks

2 4 6 8 10 9 7 5 3 1

Chapter One

The minute Wajid Haq walked through the door of Year Five's classroom, Wallace Meek felt the unmistakable "zing" that meant something exciting was going to happen.

There was a whole variety of reasons. Firstly, Wajid wore a dazzling smile that seemed to light up the whole classroom, and as soon as he saw Wallace sitting in the front seat he directed the smile at him. It made Wallace feel instantly special.

Secondly, Wajid wore an extremely smart navy-blue suit and bright white shirt, and his dark, shiny hair was combed neatly in place. Wallace, who tended to have trouble keeping his clothes and hair at all tidy, very much admired

smartness in others. He loved Wajid's style.

Thirdly, Wallace liked the confident way Wajid walked into the classroom and beamed at everyone. Wallace had been at Grimstone Primary all his life, but he was sure if he had to go to a new school he would be painfully shy on the first day. All in all, he decided, Wajid Haq had "star quality".

But there was something else. Wajid was wearing the most fascinating device. It was a small plastic box with two black wires sprouting from it, and as Wajid walked over to stand beside Miss Bannigan to be introduced, Wallace thought he could just make out a tiny flash of red light from its top.

That did it. If there was anything that turned Wallace on, it was technology! If it had wires and fuses and switches and lights, Wallace was hooked – and the little device over Wajid's shoulder was positively brimful of electronic potential. He couldn't wait to find out more!

"Let me introduce Wajid Haq, Year Five," Miss Bannigan said, smiling at everyone. "Wajid is going to join us, and I'm sure we'll all make him very welcome."

Wallace didn't waste a second. Before anyone else claimed Wajid, he put his hand up and said, "Miss Bannigan – perhaps I could show Wajid the toilets and the cloakroom later?"

"Thank you, Wallace," Miss Bannigan said gratefully. "That would be very kind."

Then, patting a small black box round her neck, she turned to Wajid. "So here we are, Wajid," she said. "We're wired for sound, aren't we!"

Wallace craned forward in his seat, pushing his glasses further up his nose, which always improved the focus. He was fascinated to see that Miss Bannigan's box, which he had  assumed all morning to be an item of ultra-modern jewellery (though not a particularly nice item of ultra-modern jewellery), had a small silver switch and a tiny green light. Things were getting even more intriguing!

"You will see, Year Five," Miss Bannigan said as Wajid carefully plugged each black wire into one of his hearing aids, "that Wajid and I are electronically connected."

That certainly made everyone sit up and take notice. Even Jasbir, who had been busy combing Melanie's hair back into a ponytail and fixing it with rose-covered hair-clips, stopped for a moment to look. And it made a shiver of excitement run right up Wallace's back.

"Wajid has trouble hearing when I'm talking to all of you," Miss Bannigan explained. "So he's got this Radio Aid which is composed of a..." She paused and wrinkled her brow. "What do you call it, Wajid?"

"A transmitter, Miss Bannigan," Wajid smiled encouragingly. "That's the box round your neck with all the controls and the inbuilt mike. And in here..." he went on, indicating his

own plastic box, "is the receiver, which I've just connected to my hearing aids. It means, Miss Bannigan, that you and I are on the same wavelength, so to speak." Then he faced the class, turning his head slowly from right to left and pointing to each plastic earpiece in turn.

"Just like a personal CD player," he explained.

Then, beaming an even more dazzling smile in Miss Bannigan's direction, he added, "But much more educational, of course."

Miss Bannigan blushed slightly, dipped her head, and said, "One ... two ... three ... testing..." very slowly and loudly into the top of the black box.

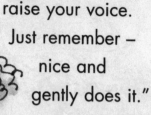

"How was that?" she asked.

"A trifle loud," Wajid smiled. "No need to raise your voice. Just remember – nice and gently does it."

Miss Bannigan, looking a little flustered, steered Wajid into the empty seat beside Wallace. "Perhaps you should sit at the front for the moment, Wajid," she said, nice and gently. "Till we get our acoustics sorted out. If there's anything you don't understand, just ask Wallace."

And that was the beginning of Wallace and Wajid's friendship.

Chapter Two

The first thing Wallace showed Wajid, after the toilets and the cloakroom, was the Special Place by the Wheelie-bins. The Special Place by the Wheelie-bins (codename: S.P.E.W.) was a spot in the playground where Wallace spent a great deal of time.

It was a small enclosed area outside the school kitchens, where the wheelie-bins gave shade in summer and shelter in winter and, since S.P.E.W. had its own very particular smell all the year round, Wallace was hardly ever disturbed there.

"Neat," Wajid smiled as Wallace held a bin aside for him to squeeze in. He squatted down, and took a banana out of his pocket. Wallace noticed gratefully that he didn't mention the smell, which today was mainly turnip with a dash of three-day-old beefburger. Wallace took out two cream crackers and they both munched happily.

"Cool that we're getting to sit together, isn't it," Wajid said at last. He had unplugged the black wires from his hearing aids, wound them up, and pushed them into his pocket, but the little red light on his receiver box still blinked on and off invitingly. Wallace was dying to have a closer look at it.

Just as he was going to ask whether he could, Wajid suddenly finished his banana, unwound the wires, plugged them in, and twiddled with something on his hearing aids. "You're at the front on account of your eyes, I presume?" he said.

Wallace nodded. "Short sight," he explained. "Can't see the board unless it's within three paces." He handed his spectacles to Wajid and held a cracker up to his left eye. "Funny thing, this," he said. "Discovered it quite by chance. If I look through one of the holes, everything's perfectly in focus."

Wajid frowned. He put Wallace's glasses on and winced. "Crikey!" he said. "These are strong. Imagine a cream cracker being just as effective – though I daresay the image is rather too small to be practical?"

"Oh yes," said Wallace, wiping the
crumbs off his nose and putting his glasses
back on. "And you must never use one with
cottage cheese on – you could end up
looking like a panda!"

They heaved with laughter for a while.

Then Wajid became very quiet and, with
a glazed look, he turned to Wallace and
said, mysteriously, "I have second sight,
you know."

"Second sight?" gasped Wallace. "Doesn't
that mean you can see into the future?"

Wajid nodded and pressed his forefingers against his temples, rubbing them with small circular movements.

For the third time that day, Wallace felt the tiny shiver of excitement. "Could you tell me something that's going to happen?" he whispered.

Wajid continued to rub for a bit. Then he started to hum.

And then he spoke, in a low, quivering voice. "Miss Ba-a-a-a-a-anigan is going to give us a ma-a-a-a-aths test as soon as we go in..."

Wallace gasped. "That is truly awesome!" he said, looking admiringly at his new friend. "You could only know that by supernatural means! We always get a maths test on a Friday morning," he went on to explain. "Twenty questions, come rain, hail or shine. Don't suppose you can tell what the questions are going to be?"

Wajid shut his eyes very tightly and continued the circular rubbing. When he spoke again, his voice was very deep and solemn.

"This is not just any old ma-a-a-a-aths test..." he intoned. "This is going to be a fo-o-o-o-o-orty-question maths test on the three, four, and five times ta-a-a-a-ables, with the occasional subtraction thrown in to keep us on our to-o-o-o-o-o-o-oes..."

Wallace sank back against the wheelie-bins. It was staggering!

"Anything else?" he whispered.

Wajid shook his head. The bell began to ring and the boys stood up and checked the backs of their trousers for stray food particles. Then they began to walk slowly to the line. As they took their places at the end, Wajid closed his eyes and gave a very short hum.

"Yes?" said Wallace eagerly.

"She's had tuna-a-a-a-a-a-a fish sandwiches for her mid-morning snack..." Wajid said, tremulously.

Chapter Three

"Now, Year Five," Miss Bannigan said as she placed a piece of paper in front of each of them. The papers were numbered down the side. "I have decided today to give you a rather special maths test."

Jasbir, who sat beside Melanie right at the back of the class, put up her hand. "But Miss Bannigan!" she said dramatically. "There are forty questions!"

"We usually only get twenty," added Melanie, sounding badly put out.

Wajid turned to Wallace and gave him the tiniest of winks.

"This is an extra-special Tables Test," Miss Bannigan told Jasbir and Melanie firmly. "It's revision." Wallace could hardly believe his ears as she explained that the questions would be on the three, four and five times tables.

"And I shall be throwing in the occasional subtraction," she went on, smiling at the rest of the class, "to keep you on your toes!"

As she passed Wallace and Wajid's seats she paused and bent over Wajid.

"How am I doing, Wajid?" she whispered. "Not too loud?"

Wajid smiled at her. "Not at all, Miss Bannigan," he said.
"Crystal clear."

Miss Bannigan gave a grateful little sigh of relief. Wallace dug his elbow into Wajid's waist and gave him a thumbs-up sign, just below the table.

When Miss Bannigan had sighed, there had been a distinct smell of tuna fish.

The test took longer than usual. Just as they reached number thirty-eight, the classroom door opened and Mr Parsons, the Year Six teacher, strode in. He was a tall man with very blond hair, very blue eyes and a lot of very white teeth. Jasbir and Melanie always giggled when he came into the classroom – which he had been doing rather often lately.

Miss Bannigan flashed him a wide smile and fluttered her pale-blue eyelids.

"Oh, Miss Bannigan," they heard Mr Parsons say, "I see you're in the middle of something important – I'll come back later..." And he turned to go.

Everyone in Year Five put down their pencils and watched, grateful for something to take them away from number thirty-eight. It was a particularly horrible subtraction which, rather than keeping them on their toes, was bringing most of them to their knees. Miss Bannigan looked round the class. "Has everyone finished number thirty-eight?" she asked.

A few people shook their heads, but Miss Bannigan ignored them. "Turn your papers over. I have an important matter to discuss with Mr Parsons. On no account look at your neighbour's work, or discuss any of your answers."

And she and Mr Parsons began to whisper to one another. Every now and then Miss Bannigan looked round the class, occasionally frowning at someone whose lip had twitched.

Wallace leaned back in his seat and watched Wajid out of the corner of his eye. Wajid was leaning on his elbows with his head down and his hands clamped over his ears. Finally, unable to bear the tension any longer, Wallace wrote:

CAN YOU HEAR WHAT THEY
ARE TALKING ABOUT?

on the piece of scrap paper Miss Bannigan always provided for rough working, and carefully slid it round Wajid's elbow and under his nose.

After what seemed like an eternity Wajid
wrote something very slowly and neatly, and
slipped the piece of paper back to Wallace.

Wallace read Wajid's note and frowned.
Sure enough, Miss Bannigan did look really
worried. She kept shaking her head and
pulling at her earrings, and
Mr Parsons kept
patting her
arm. It
was
really
very
upsetting.

Wallace went on watching Wajid, wondering if he would reveal any more details, but Wajid began to check each of the answers on his test sheet. As he did, he rubbed his temples in small circular movements just as he had done when he had demonstrated his powers of second sight.

Then the penny dropped. Suddenly Wallace had a strong feeling that the "second sight" business wasn't as impressive as it had seemed, after all.

It didn't, he thought rather ruefully, take a cream cracker to see through Wajid Haq.

Chapter Four

The conversation between Miss Bannigan and Mr Parsons lasted quite a long time, and Miss Bannigan kept on pulling at her earrings and twisting her little black curls round her fingers. At one point she rushed over to the cupboard where she kept the textbooks and took out a copy of *Spelling Made Simple*, which she handed to Mr Parsons.

Spelling Made Simple was a horrid book full of thousands of really difficult words and very boring sentences with gaps to fit the really difficult words into. Miss Bannigan always gave it out on a Monday morning and Wallace's heart sank every time he saw its faded blue cover. It was the fattest little book Wallace had ever seen, so there seemed no chance of ever getting to the end of it, and every copy had dog-eared pages which were yellowed with age and smelt of mould.

Wallace drummed his fingers on his desk in frustration. There was really no accounting for teachers, he thought. How could two adults spend five minutes leafing through a book that just had lists and lists of difficult words?

And what on earth was worrying poor Miss Bannigan?

Finally, Mr Parsons moved towards the door and said, in a very loud and jolly voice, "At lunchtime, then – we'll sort it out once and for all, shall we?" Then he beamed a very white smile all round the classroom and off he went.

Miss Bannigan stood for a while with the spelling book, flicking through it and reading bits, then sighing deeply and

shaking her head. Finally she thumped it down on her desk, picked up her test paper, and carried on with number thirty-nine as though nothing at all had happened.

When they swapped papers and marked their tests, Wallace was impressed to see that Wajid had done extremely well.

He had even got number thirty-eight right, and Wallace was once more overcome with admiration. Not only did Wajid have second sight, he was also a Maths Wizard!

Except that, of course, Wallace wasn't at all sure that he believed the "second sight" business any more. At lunchtime, back at S.P.E.W., he tackled Wajid.

"About your 'second sight', Wajid..." he began, not quite knowing how to put it without sounding rude. "You can't really see into the future, can you? It's that Radio Aid, isn't it?"

Wajid unpacked his lunchbox and handed Wallace a large corner of vegetable samosa. Wallace accepted it gratefully and gave him two spring onions in return.

"Course I can't!" Wajid laughed. "Miss Bannigan forgot to switch it off, so I heard her talking in the staffroom. It's a good trick, though, isn't it?" He gazed into the distance, and went on dreamily. "I once thought of doing it professionally, you know – charging people money to have their fortunes told.

Thought I'd set up a little booth and wear gold earrings and a spotted scarf round my head, and put up a big gold sign with: *The Future Foretold by Wajid the Wise – 20p.*

"I'd have an accomplice of course – planted outside, feeding me information. And if we got really good at it we might actually become famous and get a show on television."

"What a cunning idea!" said Wallace. "I'll be your accomplice if you like," he added eagerly.

But Wajid shook his head. "No, Wallace – thanks for offering, but I gave up the idea a while ago. It would be terribly dishonest.

"I still want to be famous, though!" he went on, his brown eyes shining. "You mark my words, Wallace – one of these days I'll wear an evening suit and my name'll be up in lights!"

Wallace closed his eyes for a moment, imagining Wajid in top hat and tails standing under a huge sign made up of very bright lightbulbs that flashed on and off and spelled out *Wajid the Wise*, and then *Wajid the Wonderful* in a dozen different colours. It made the hairs on the back of his neck stand up on end.

"Tell you what, though, Wallace," Wajid interrupted his train of thought, "if Miss Bannigan keeps forgetting to switch off, it could be very ... interesting, if you get my drift." And he tapped the side of his nose knowingly and winked.

The fourth tiny shiver of excitement zinged through Wallace. "I wish we could help Miss Bannigan with her Worry," he said, looking rather upset. "Do you think she's pretty?" he asked Wajid suddenly.

Wajid took a large mouthful of chocolate-flavoured milk and nodded. "Course!" he said. "And what's more, I think Mr Parsons thinks she's pretty too."

Wallace considered this. "Do you?" he asked, looking even more upset.

Wajid nodded. "Made for each other, I'd say," he said wisely, sucking the last drops of chocolate milk very noisily up the straw and flicking the empty carton into the nearest wheelie-bin. "And you know what they say, Wallace," he added solemnly. "A problem shared is a problem halved."

Wallace smiled bravely. He wasn't at all convinced that it was.

Chapter Five

For a while Wallace sat quietly beside
Wajid, deep in his worried thoughts. Then he
said, tentatively, "Don't suppose I could ...
have a listen?"

Wajid hesitated.

"You're not really supposed to..." he
began.

"I let you try my specs," Wallace pointed
out.

"OK then," said Wajid, rather reluctantly taking out the left hearing aid and handing it to Wallace, who held it up to his ear.

"Turn the volume up if you like," Wajid said. "It's that tiny little plastic wheel on the top."

Wallace, fascinated, twiddled for a while. Then he moved his head right up against Wajid's and they huddled together and listened. For a while, they heard nothing but crackles. Then, quite clearly, Miss Bannigan's voice rang out, high and breathless. She sounded terribly agitated.

"It's just not right in this day and age," she was saying. "You saw them for yourself this morning, didn't you? You saw my problem…"

Then Mr Parsons took over, sounding very comforting. "There, there, Amanda – or may I call you Mandy?"

Wajid glanced at Wallace and raised one eyebrow. They both covered their ears with their hands and concentrated hard.

"You've hit the nail on the head, Mandy," Mr Parsons went on. "Thick, smelly, and as dull as ditchwater – that's what they are!"

Wajid squirmed round so he was facing Wallace. "Thick and smelly?" he repeated, horrified. "That's our class he's talking about, Wallace!"

"Surely not!" Wallace said, frowning. "He wouldn't..."

"He would," said Wajid. "You heard him! I saw the way he looked at us when he came in – he could see we were struggling with number thirty-eight. He thinks Year Five's as thick as mince and as dull as ditchwater!"

"He can't possibly think we're all smelly, though..." Wallace lifted his arm and gave his armpit a quick sniff. "Maybe it's me bringing in fumes from S.P.E.W., do you think?"

"Listen!" hissed Wajid. "She's on again. Surely Miss Bannigan doesn't think her class is thick and smelly as well...?"

But, sadly, it sounded as though Miss Bannigan did.

"Yes ... of course, Peter, that's it in a nutshell..." she was saying, her voice suddenly much calmer. "They're not a patch on the ones I had in my last school, you know. They were so bright and interesting, and not half as thick. And they didn't stink to high heaven either!"

There was a pause, during which Wallace and Wajid stared at each other in horrified silence.

At last Mr Parsons spoke again, and his voice sounded like the very knell of doom.

"Quite honestly, Mandy, I think you should chuck them all out. Pick out the really thick smelly ones, and throw them in the bin! You shouldn't have to put up with them in your classroom a moment longer, you know.

"Who knows, Mandy," he went on, his voice so high now it was almost a squeak, "they might even be a health hazard!"

"You're right, Peter," Miss Bannigan's voice said calmly and decisively. "The bin's the place for them. Let's choose which ones are worst, right now!"

Wallace and Wajid clutched one another.
Together, they glanced behind them at the
red plastic wheelie-bins which had been
Wallace's refuge in all his hours of need.
Then they unplugged the black wires
forlornly, and let them slip down to lie limply
in their laps.

Chapter Six

"I feel betrayed, Wajid," said Wallace at last, handing Wajid back his left hearing aid. "I worshipped the very ground Miss Bannigan trod on, you know."

He took off his glasses and wiped them on his sleeve. "I can see clearly now," he said, putting them back on. "She's a snake in the grass."

Wajid nodded. "Just proves what I've always said," he sighed. "You should never trust a pretty teacher…"

And they sank back sadly against the wheelie-bins and thought gloomy thoughts.

After a moment Wajid sat bolt upright.

"I have had a terrible thought, Wallace," he said, solemnly. "Know what I reckon they're off planning right now?"

"What?" said Wallace.

"I reckon they're off to prepare the MOTHER OF ALL TESTS, to find out who's really thick. And everyone that fails this test will be..."

"...thrown in the bin..." squeaked Wallace.

"We've got to warn everyone!" said Wajid, suddenly leaping into action. "Come on, Wallace! There's no time to lose!" and he ran round to the main part of the playground. Wallace, however, hung back and stood for a moment looking very thoughtfully at the wheelie-bins.

When Wajid arrived, panting, at the spot where Year Five tended to gather, most of the class had formed a little half-circle round Jasbir and Melanie, who were competing in the *World's Longest Handstand* competition against the wall.

They were all counting in unison, and had just reached one hundred and three when Wajid pushed his way through and stood, silent, his arms flapping up and down. For quite a while his mouth opened and closed but no sound came out.

Wallace joined him and pulled at his sleeve. "Hang on, Wajid," he hissed. "We may not be in full possession of the facts, you know..."

"Course we are," Wajid hissed back. "We heard it with our own ears..."

"We may be leaping to conclusions..." Wallace went on miserably. "Please don't panic everyone..."

"Course I won't panic them," Wajid assured him. He cupped his hands and raised them to his mouth, and then he shouted in a voice that would have wakened the dead:

"BE WARNED BY WAJID THE WISE! A MOST TERRIBLE THING IS ABOUT TO HAPPEN – WE'RE GOING TO GET THE MOTHER OF ALL TESTS!"

Suddenly, an eerie silence filled the playground as everyone looked at each other in horror. Then Melanie yelled furiously "Don't listen to him!" and Jasbir, her face very red, added, "Ignore *Wajid the Wise* – keep counting!"

A few voices half-heartedly began again, but most of Year Five stood, thunderstruck, waiting for another announcement.

"Honestly!" Wajid went on, pointing at his Radio Aid. "We heard it! Miss Bannigan thinks we're thick and smelly and as dull as ditchwater so she's going to give us a terrible test, and everyone who fails this test will be..."

" ...put in the bin," finished Wallace unhappily. He looked at Wajid and wrinkled his brow. "Wajid," he whispered out of the corner of his mouth, "I'm not at all sure..."

But Wajid had the bit between his teeth, and there was no stopping him.

"Swot up your parts of speech!" he roared. "Learn your tables right up to twelve times! Leave no stone unturned!"

Almost everyone rushed off in a panic to fetch their books, but Jasbir and Melanie, now upright, stood their ground. "We were at a hundred and seventeen!" they chorused, each taking hold of one of Wajid's arms and pushing him back and forth between them.

"We could have stayed up till two hundred!" they went on, beside themselves with rage. "We could have beaten the World Record if it wasn't for you, you bampot!"

"Look," Wajid said, trying to shake them off, "this is a dire emergency. It's for your own good. You don't want to be thrown in the bin, do you?"

"Bin my foot," Jasbir growled. "You're off your head, Wajid Haq. As if Wallace Meek wasn't bad enough with all his weird ideas..." And she stomped off to make another handstand attempt.

Wallace and Wajid fetched their schoolbags from the cloakroom and huddled back into S.P.E.W. Wajid began reciting his tables, and Wallace leafed through his spelling exercise book, making sure he could spell "because" and "encyclopaedia". Soon, the playground was filled with little groups of feverishly swotting children.

Only Jasbir and Melanie stood stolidly on their hands, watching them all with utter disdain.

Chapter Seven

When the bell rang, Year Five trailed back
into school with their noses still in their
books. All that could be heard from their side
of the cloakroom were panicky whispers:

"How many continents are there?"

"What's an adverb?"

"How many nines in eighty-one?"

When they got to the classroom, though, there were no test papers waiting for them. In fact, there was no teacher, and after five minutes all eyes turned to Wallace and Wajid.

"Well?" said Melanie.

"Where is it then?" said Jasbir. "Where's the 'Mother of all Tests'?"

Wajid shot Wallace an uncomfortable glance and handed him the left hearing aid. Everyone gathered round.

"What can you hear?" said Melanie, trying not to sound too interested.

"Sssssh!" said Wajid. "Miss Bannigan's obviously on the move..."

A great deal of rustling echoed through Radio Aid and then, quite distinctly, they heard Miss Bannigan's voice. Wallace clasped his hand round Wajid's upper arm and dug the nails in hard.

"Listen!" he hissed. "She's coming in loud and clear ... and she sounds as if she's somewhere big and echoey!"

"Probably the Ministry of Tests," said Wajid, his voice deep with gloom.

Everyone edged even closer to Wallace and Wajid and watched with bated breath.

"I reckon she's in a cupboard," Wallace whispered. "It's sort of muffled."

Wallace pressed his right ear hard against Wajid's head to deaden the background sounds, and said "Shhhhh!" again just to make sure. Then, sounding as though it came from a goldfish bowl, they heard Miss Bannigan's voice.

"*Spelling Without Tears*... Oh, Peter, these are much better! Modern, colourful, full of beautiful illustrations. They'll be a joy to use!"

Then they heard the deeper and more strident voice of Mr Parsons.

"Right you are, Mandy – we'll get rid of the old ones and get you a nice class set of these..."

Wallace and Wajid looked at one another. Wallace could feel his face turning pink.

"Now just let me sque-e-e-eze over and get them down, Mandy," Mr Parsons was saying. "Here we are – twenty-eight lovely new books!"

"Oh, thank you so much, Peter," Miss Bannigan replied. "They're much more my style! Now watch you don't drop them..."

Wallace gulped.

"What are they saying, Wajid Haq?" Melanie shouted. "Are they in the Ministry of Tests?"

"Er..." Wajid began. "Not exactly..." He covered his face with his hands and squinted through a small gap between his fingers. "They're in the ... book cupboard," he said quietly.

"Getting spelling books," Wallace added.

Twenty-six pairs of eyes stared at them.
You could almost smell the anger.
"Sorry…" said Wallace, humbly.
"Got our lines crossed," said Wajid.
"Easy mistake to make," Wallace pointed out.
"James Bond's always doing it," observed
Wajid.
And they both smiled apologetically,
and went on listening.

Chapter Eight

Wallace and Wajid listened on, their faces growing pinker and pinker. In the book cupboard, things had taken an unusual turn.

"Mandy ... I was wondering..." Mr Parsons said hesitantly, and Miss Bannigan rather breathlessly answered, "Yes, Peter?"

"I'm very keen on bell-ringing," Mr Parsons went on, "and I was wondering whether you might do me the honour of accompanying me this evening...?"

"Oh, Peter!" Miss Bannigan sighed. "That would be absolutely lovely..."

"Come on," said Jasbir, getting up and motioning to everyone else to follow her. "They're just a waste of space, those two."

"A World Record ruined," added Melanie scathingly. "For nothing." And one by one everyone drifted back to their seats.

"Listen!" said Wallace suddenly. "I heard a crash!"

Sure enough, there was suddenly a great deal of scuffling coming over the airwaves. Then Mr Parsons' voice said, "Oh, I am clumsy. Are you all right, Mandy ... dear?"

"I can't bear this," said Wajid. "Makes me feel sick."

"Keep listening," Wallace insisted. "You need a strong stomach for this kind of work, you know."

There was a great deal more scuffling, after which Mr Parsons said, "Oh no! I can't believe it. This is dreadful!" Then all was still.

Wallace and Wajid stared, horrified, at one another. "Oh my goodness!" whispered Wallace. "We've lost the connection. Something has gone terribly wrong."

They turned up the volume to maximum, pressed their hands hard against the hearing aids, and listened. Suddenly, to their relief, they heard Miss Bannigan's voice again.

"It's completely stuck!" she was saying. "The door won't open, Peter!"

"Now, don't panic, Mandy," Mr Parsons told her calmly. "It's my silly fault, reversing into the door handle with this pile of books. All it needs is a jolly good rattle..."

The sound of two teachers giving a cupboard door a jolly good rattle travelled down the airwaves.

"They're stuck!" Wallace breathed. "Miss Bannigan and Mr Parsons are stuck in the book cupboard ... together!"

A few people looked across at him with interest.

"Don't pay any attention to him," said Melanie.

"But we have to do something," said Wajid.

"Or him," said Jasbir, through gritted teeth. "They're making it all up. No one leaves this classroom, and that's an order. Miss Bannigan expects us to sit quietly like little mice. So Meek and Haq, you sit quietly, like little mice, or else. Understood?"

"B-b-but," whispered Wajid, "we can't just leave them..."

But Jasbir gave him a dangerous look. "That's my last word," she said.

Wallace looked miserably at Wajid, and Wajid looked miserably back at Wallace. Finally Wallace mouthed, "I bet I know what James Bond would do..."

And Wajid nodded and said, "I bet I do too."

So saying, they rose and, still connected by the black wires, shuffled out of the classroom to the shrill sounds of Jasbir and Melanie's warnings.

"Just you wait! You've done it now!"

Chapter Nine

When Wallace and Wajid got to the
caretaker's room, the door was closed and
it had a big *Do Not Disturb* notice on it.
Faintly, from inside, they could hear the
results of the last race from Newmarket.

"Mr Grubb! Emergency! Open up,
please!" Wallace yelled.

There was a click and silence, followed
by a great deal of heaving and groaning
as Mr Grubb pulled himself out of his plastic
chair and opened the door. He looked very
far from pleased.

"What the devil's this?" he said, looking
at the black wires leading out of their ears.
"MI 5?"

"Please, Mr Grubb..." Wallace spluttered,
almost incoherent with panic. "Our
teacher's stuck in the book cupboard with
Mr Parsons..."

"Goodness knows how much air's in there,"
Wajid added. "Speed is of the essence!"

"Is it, indeed?" said Mr Grubb. "Well, you'll just have to hang on till I find the right key..." and he searched very slowly through the bunch that hung from his trouser pocket.

"Come on!" shouted Wallace, detaching himself from Wajid for safety's sake. "Follow us and look for it on the way!"

With difficulty, Wallace and Wajid led Mr Grubb upstairs. When they reached the door that said BOOK CUPBOARD – STAFF ONLY, the radio line was dead, but through the door they could hear little thumps and a weak cry of "Let us out!"

"Oh my goodness me," said Mr Grubb. "Why didn't you tell me sooner?" And he went on looking through the collection of keys.

"It's all right!" Wallace called. "Help is at hand!"

"We're almost out of air!" Mr Parsons' voice told them thinly. "Hurry up!"

"Breathe through the keyhole!" shouted Wajid.

"Here it is!" said Mr Grubb at last, pushing the key in the lock.

It took a great deal of twiddling, but finally the cupboard door opened and an avalanche of books of all sizes and descriptions tumbled out. Miss Bannigan and Mr Parsons followed, both very pale and each clutching a bundle of *Spelling Without Tears* to their chests.

"Oh my goodness!" said Mr Parsons, wiping his brow with his handkerchief. "I'm not at all good in confined spaces."

When they saw Wallace and Wajid, they looked extremely embarrassed; and when Wajid tapped the Radio Aid and said quietly, "You'll find it's best to turn it off when not in use," they looked at one another in dismay.

"You mean..." Miss Bannigan said, looking in horror at the transmitter box. "You've been listening...?"

Her face went bright red, and her little black curls seemed to stand right out on end like corkscrews. Wallace looked at Wajid and gave him a wink, praying that he would understand.

"No, no..." Wajid said quickly, returning the wink. "We just heard vague noises, that was all..."

"It's not really all that sensitive," added Wallace. "Not when the transmitter and the receiver are far apart."

"Especially in a cupboard," said Wajid.

"Can't hear a thing from cupboards," agreed Wallace.

"Hardly anything," they smiled together.

Miss Bannigan brightened up. "Perhaps we should be getting back to the classroom now?" she smiled. "Give out the new spelling books?"

"Of course, Miss Bannigan," said Wallace. "Can I help you carry them?"

They all set off with their piles of *Spelling Without Tears*.

As they reached the bottom of the stairs Mr Parsons, still looking very upset, dropped his books and Wallace and Wajid left Miss Bannigan and ran back to help him pick them up.

"There we are, sir," said Wallace as he balanced the final book on the top of Mr Parsons' trembling pile. "That seems much less shaky."

"Thank you, Wallace," said Mr Parsons, peering round the books with a troubled frown. "Now come along, we really must hurry back to class. The bell's long overdue."

Wallace winked at Wajid again.

"Wajid..." he said. "You didn't hear the bell ringing, did you?"

They both smiled innocently at Mr Parsons, and then Wajid rubbed his temples with very slow, circular movements.

"Oh y-e-e-e-e-e-es," he murmured mystically. "I definitely heard the b-e-l-l r-i-n-g-i-n-g,"

Then he and Wallace aimed a final, unmistakable, wink in the direction of Mr Parsons.